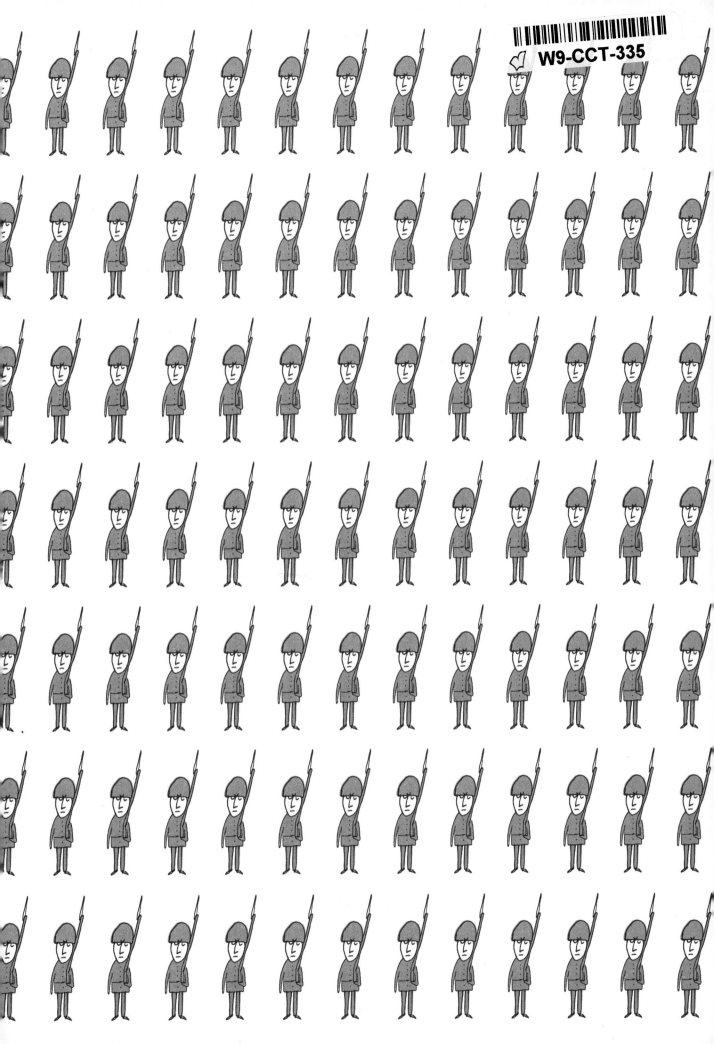

W9-CCT-335

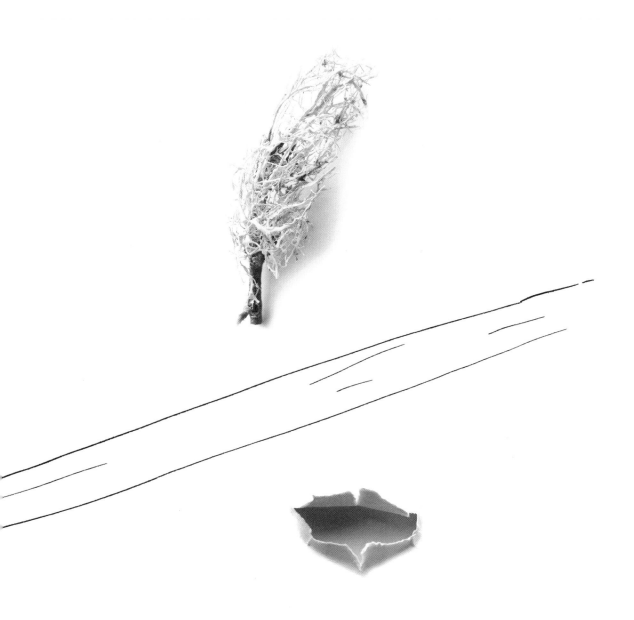

Look. Do you see two holes?

Look more closely. Do you see the soldiers in those holes?

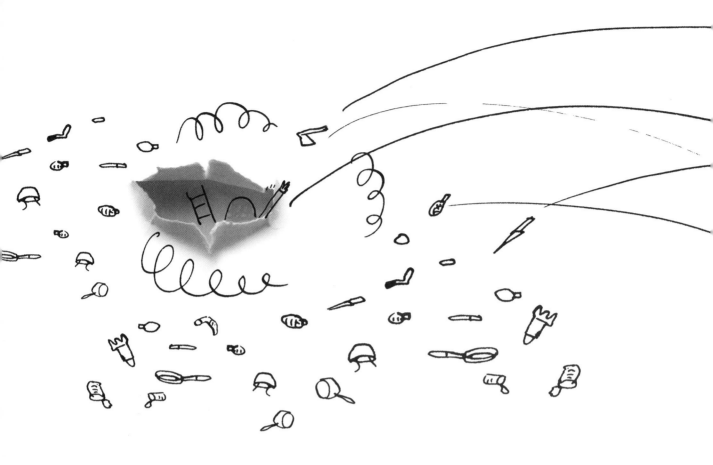

They are enemies.

Published by Schwartz & Wade Books
an imprint of Random House Children's Books
a division of Random House, Inc., New York

Translation copyright © 2009 by Éditions Sarbacane

All rights reserved.

Schwartz & Wade Books and the colophon are trademarks of Random House, Inc.

Originally published in France as L'Ennemi by Éditions Sarbacane, Paris,
copyright © 2007 by Éditions Sarbacane, Paris, in 2007.

Visit us on the Web! www.randomhouse.com/kids

Educators and librarians, for a variety of teaching tools, visit us at
www.randomhouse.com/teachers

Library of Congress Cataloging-in-Publication Data
Cali, Davide.
[L'ennemi. English]
The enemy / by Davide Cali ; illustrated by Serge Bloch. —
1st ed.
p. cm.
Summary: After watching an enemy for a very long time during an endless war,
a soldier finally creeps out into the night to the other man's hole and is surprised
by what he finds there.
ISBN 978-0-375-84500-0 (trade)
ISBN 978-0-375-93752-1 (Gibraltar lib. bdg.)
[1. Soldiers—Fiction. 2. War—Fiction. 3. Enemies (Persons)—Fiction.]
I. Bloch, Serge, ill. II. Title.
PZ7.C1283Ene 2009
[E]—dc22
2007047974

The text of this book is set in Graham.
The illustrations are rendered in China ink on paper and photography.

PRINTED IN CHINA • 10 9 8 7 6 5 4 3 2

Random House Children's Books supports the First Amendment and celebrates the right to read.

the ENEMY

a book about peace

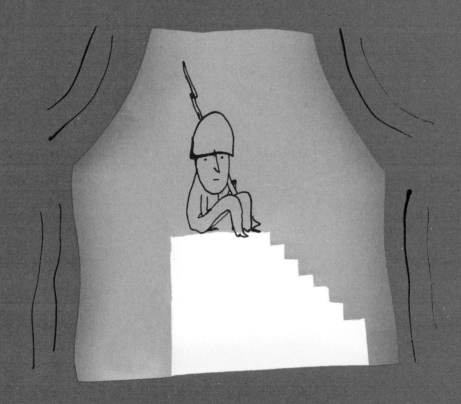

written by **DAVIDE CALI** and illustrated by **SERGE BLOCH**

schwartz & wade books · new york

The enemy is there but I have never seen him.
Every morning, I shoot at him. Then he shoots at me.

We both stay hidden the rest of the day, waiting.

Even when I'm hungry, I wait. I do not make a cooking fire.
The enemy could sneak up when I'm not looking and kill me.

But sometimes I am so hungry I light my fire.

As soon as I do, the enemy lights his.

Except for hunger, the enemy and I have nothing in common. He is a wild beast. He does not know mercy. I know this because I read it in my manual.

A long time ago, on the first day of the war, we were given a manual and a gun. The manual tells us everything about the enemy. It says that we must kill him before he kills us.

If he kills us, he will also kill our families and our pets, burn down our forests, even poison our water. The enemy is not a human being.

Sometimes I think the others have forgotten us. Maybe the war is over and no one remembered to tell us. Or maybe the world does not exist anymore.

Maybe we are the last two soldiers fighting. Maybe whichever one of us survives will win the war.

I have almost nothing to eat. Once I nearly caught a lizard that came close to my hole. Then I thought, "If he sees me eating a lizard, the enemy will think I am desperate."

Luckily, there is water from the well. I must be watchful—
the enemy could poison it when I'm not looking.

At night, there are lots of stars above my hole. I wonder if the enemy sees them too. Maybe if he looked at them he would understand that war is pointless and it must stop.

But I can't be the first to stop fighting, because he
would kill me. I would not kill him if he stopped first,
because I am a man. I am not a beast.

It is raining again and I hate the rain. The war needs to end because I cannot stay in this hole any longer. Last night the beating of the rain kept me awake. As I sat, I thought that soon there won't be a moon. If I leave my hole then, the enemy won't be able to see me.

I thought, "Soon the war could end."

At last it is time. I put on Disguise Number Three—the bush—and leave.

It is chilly but the disguise keeps me warm. I crawl toward the enemy's hole to surprise him. I am going to kill him. Then the war will be over and I can go home to my family.

I have made a mistake. There are lions at night, and they can see in the dark. I just spotted one and must stay still.

I am lucky. The lion is leaving.

At last I reach the enemy's hole—but no one
is here! He *must* be here! His things are here.
There are pictures of his family. . . .
I wasn't expecting him to have a family.

And what's this? A manual just like mine. But there is a difference: in this one, the enemy has my face.

This manual is full of lies—I am a man, not a monster. I am not the one who started this war.

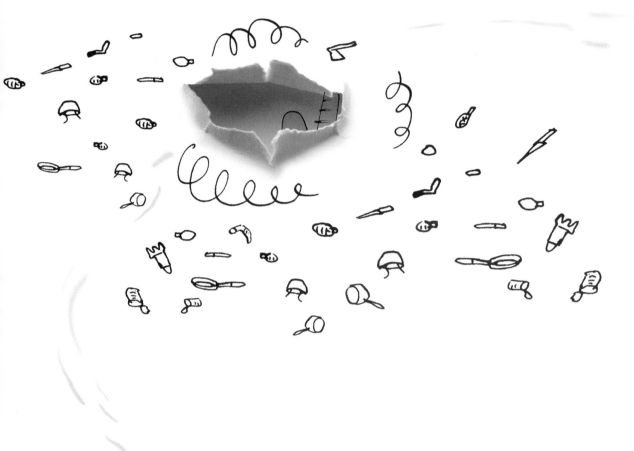

It is near dawn and there is no sign of the enemy. Suddenly, I know where he is—he is in my hole! He tried to sneak up on me to end the war. Now I can't leave his hole.

If only he would send me a message saying, "Let's end the war now." I would agree to it right away. So what is he waiting for?

I am tired of waiting. There are clouds in the sky.
It is going to rain again and I hate the rain.

I write a message on a handkerchief and put it in
a plastic bottle.

I close the bottle, aim carefully, and throw it.

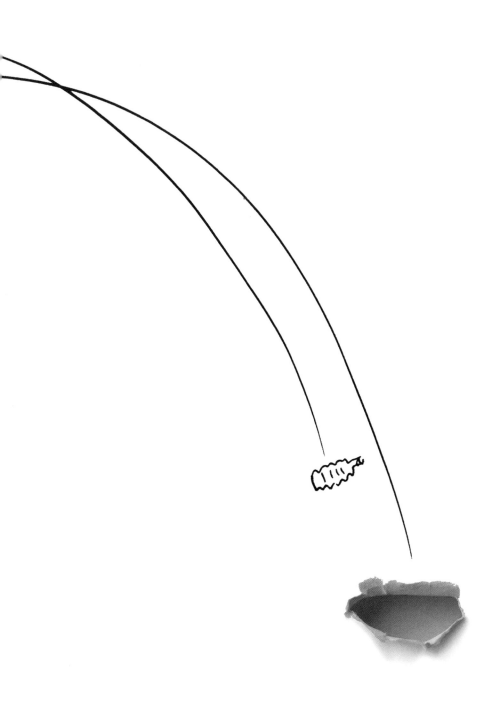

I hope my bottle falls in his hole.

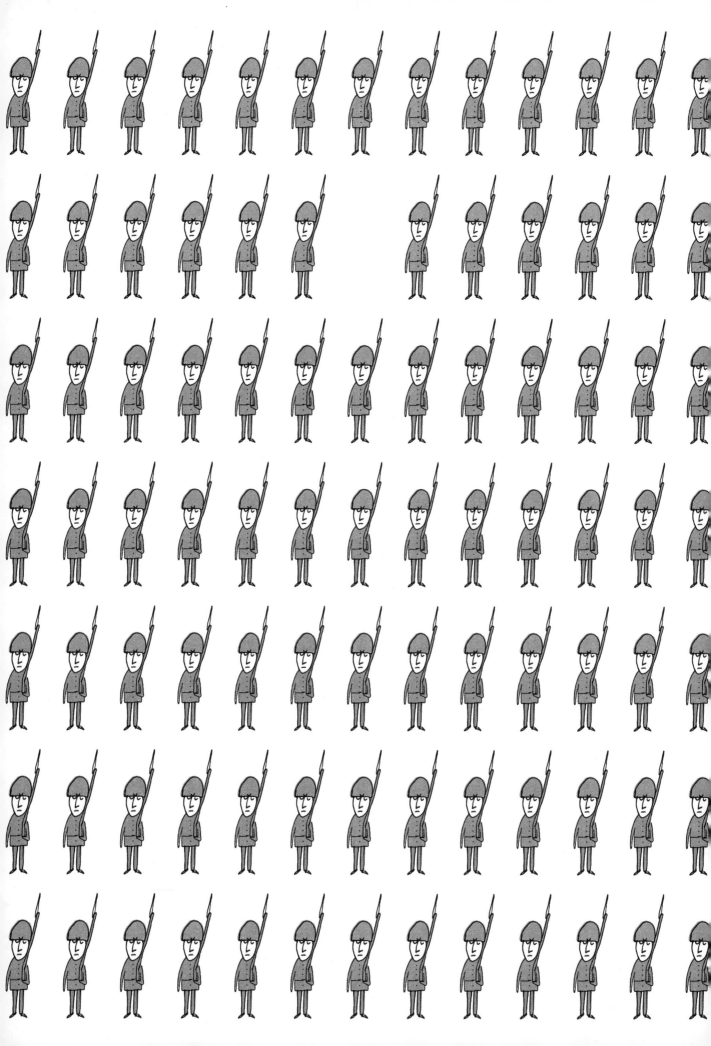